The
Secret
On The
Wall

Pam Zollman

Illustrated by Peter Fasolino

STECK-VAUGHN
ELEMENTARY · SECONDARY · ADULT · LIBRARY

A Harcourt Company

www.steck-vaughn.com

ISBN 0-7398-5135-7

Contents

Chapter 1

Strange Scribbles

It was the summer of 1890, and the knock at my door was the first of many surprises.

"Why didn't you invite me for cake, John?" Helen Holmes asked. "I want to meet your cousins."

I was so surprised that I couldn't speak for a minute. Recently, my family had moved next door to Helen's family, and Helen and I had quickly become best friends. Her uncle was the famous detective, Sherlock Holmes, and Helen was always deducing things the same way he did. I hadn't told Helen my cousins had arrived, and I had no idea how she knew we were eating cake.

"Trevor and Lizzie just arrived, and Mother did make a cake," I said. "How did you know?"

"It's simple," Helen said. "Uncle Sherlock taught me to observe. Last week, you said your cousins would be visiting. Half an hour ago, I heard a carriage pass my house." She pointed to my shirt. "The icing on your collar is from your mother's chocolate cake. She only makes that cake for guests. Your cousins must be the guests."

"Amazing," I said, as I wiped my collar.

Helen smiled. "Besides, I smelled the cake baking as I walked by this morning."

I laughed. "Mother saved you a piece. Come meet Trevor and Lizzie."

In the dining room, five-year-old Lizzie had icing on her cheeks. Cake crumbs decorated the tablecloth by her plate.

Trevor stared out the window, his cake untouched. My cousin was 14, a year younger than Helen and me. He was tall and clumsy, always tripping over his huge feet.

2

I made the introductions. Trevor was tearing a piece of paper to shreds. He nodded hello, then turned to my mother. "May I be excused? I don't feel well."

Mother felt his forehead. "You don't have a fever, but you do look pale."

"I'm tired," Trevor said. "I'll go lie down."

"Of course," Mother said. She beckoned to Lizzie. "Let's wash that messy face." Lizzie protested as Mother led her into the kitchen.

Helen and I chatted until Lizzie raced out of the kitchen, giggling. Mother followed, chasing her around the dining table.

"Go outside if you want to run," Mother said sternly. "And stop being mischievous." She marched Lizzie through the kitchen, and we heard the back door open and close.

I rolled my eyes. "I hope this isn't what my summer will be like."

Helen asked, "Your cousins are staying for the whole summer? Are their parents gone?"

"No. Trevor begged my Aunt Julia to let him visit," I explained. "Lizzie wanted to come, too."

"You look disappointed," Helen said. "Aren't you glad they're here?"

"I am," I said. "But Trevor and I wanted to go fishing today. He must be tired from the trip."

"It's only an hour's ride from Trevor's town," Helen said. "He shouldn't be that tired. He seemed distracted."

We heard the back door open again as Mother went outside. Suddenly, she shouted, "What have you done?"

Helen held the back door open for me, and we found Mother scolding Lizzie in the garden. Childish chalk marks covered the garden wall.

Lizzie stared at the chalk in her hand. "I didn't do it. I just picked up the chalk," she said, starting to cry.

"Now, Lizzie—" Mother shook her head.

Lizzie wailed, "I only wanted to copy it."

"It's just Lizzie's mischief," Mother told us. "You two go back inside."

Helen and I looked at each other. "Let's see how Trevor's feeling," I suggested.

We went back inside and down the hall to my room. Trevor was lying on the extra bed near the window. The draperies were drawn, and the room was dark.

"Who was shouting?" he asked.

"It was Mother," I said. "Lizzie's in trouble."

"Again? What did she do now?"

Helen said, "She scribbled on the garden wall."

"Mother is making her wash it off," I added.

"She . . . scribbled?" Trevor sat up. "Has she started cleaning it yet?"

My windows faced the backyard. I moved the draperies aside, and I could see Mother and Lizzie pumping water into a bucket. "They're getting ready," I said.

"I'll help!" Trevor jumped out of bed and raced out of my room.

"He must be feeling better," I said.

Helen frowned. "Hmmm" was all she said.

Chapter 2

Making Mischief

That night, I convinced Trevor to go fishing with me the next day. In the morning, we went out into the garden, but we stopped when we saw Mother scolding Lizzie again.

More chalk drawings were scrawled across the wall. Lizzie was crying that she was innocent, but Mother didn't believe her.

"I'll clean it up," Trevor offered quickly.

"No," Mother said. "Lizzie will clean it up, and she'll stay in her room the rest of the day."

Trevor broke a twig off a tree branch by the wall, then snapped it into tiny pieces. "I guess I'll stay inside today, too," he said, looking unhappy. He started walking to the house.

"Lizzie's the one being punished!" I called after him. He didn't turn around.

Later, I told Helen about this puzzling incident.

"Why is it so puzzling?" she asked.

"Mother hid all the chalk yesterday," I said. "Where did Lizzie find another piece?"

Helen rubbed her chin. "Interesting. Do you remember what the drawings looked like?"

I shrugged. "Some trees, a house, a man, and a lot of stray marks. Why?"

"I'm curious, that's all," Helen said. "Can you draw them just as they appeared on the wall?" She handed me her notebook.

"Yes! I have an excellent memory," I said.

I closed my eyes for a minute, then sketched what I'd seen that morning.

"Mother's furious, and Lizzie's sulking," I said. "Trevor's upset and won't go fishing."

"I bet he doesn't want to go anywhere," Helen said. "And Lizzie says she didn't do it?"

I frowned. "Yes. What do you know that you're not telling me?"

"Nothing. I'm only guessing," she answered. "Let's talk Trevor into that fishing trip."

∿

Trevor finally agreed but said we should leave early the next morning. He said that we could catch more worms and that the fishing would be better.

At sunrise, Trevor walked behind me as I rolled quietly down the hall. Everyone else was still asleep. When Helen met us outside, we went to the garden to dig worms.

What we saw stopped us in our tracks. On the garden wall were more drawings! Trevor turned pale and looked nervously around.

"Are you all right?" I asked.

"I see Lizzie hasn't learned her lesson yet,"
Trevor mumbled. "I . . . I'd better clean this up
before Aunt Margaret sees it."

As Helen quickly copied the drawings into her
notebook, Trevor ran to the pump. He soaked a
handkerchief and used it to scrub the wall.

"Poor Lizzie!" he said. "I have to get rid of
these marks before there's more trouble."

"Lizzie couldn't have done it," I said. "She's been in her room since yesterday morning."

Trevor glanced all around the yard, then clutched his middle. "I don't feel like fishing anymore. My stomach hurts." He hurried into the house as Helen and I stared after him.

"I don't understand it," I said. "Trevor and I have always been able to tell each other everything. There's something wrong . . . I know it. Why isn't he confiding in me anymore?"

"We'll know when we crack the code," Helen said, concentrating on her notebook.

"What are you talking about? What code?" I looked more closely at her notebook.

"These drawings are repeated as if they're in a pattern," she explained. "They'll appear again. When they do, please copy them down exactly."

"I'll feel silly," I complained.

"You won't feel silly when we figure out the code," Helen replied.

Chapter 3

Cracking the Code

The next morning, scribbles appeared again on the garden wall, as Helen had predicted. Mother threatened to send Lizzie home. Trevor was still acting nervous, and I didn't know why.

I copied the drawings and took them to Helen's house.

"I think you're right," I said. "There's a pattern to the symbols. It must be a code."

Helen answered, "When I first saw the drawings, they reminded me of one of my uncle's famous cases. His friend Watson called it 'The Adventure of the Dancing Men.'"

I nodded. "I remember that case. Sherlock Holmes found messages that used stick figures with their arms and legs in different positions. Each figure stood for a letter of the alphabet."

Helen tapped the drawings in her notebook. "There's a stick figure here, too, but its arms and legs are in the same position every time. And there are lots of other symbols."

"Where do we start?" I asked.

"Uncle Sherlock taught me that the most common letter in the English language is *E*," she answered. "So the symbol for *E* will be the one used most often. Which is it?"

I studied the pictures and scratched my head. "There are a lot of trees and suns . . . but what about those strange marks that look like arrows and lines?" I asked. I counted the marks. "The slash going down to the left is the most common."

Helen smiled. "So that slash stands for the letter *E*. Let's start with the first message. There are spaces between groups of symbols, and there are five groups. We'll assume there are five words in this message. The first word starts with a tree and then has a slash standing for the second letter."

"*Blank . . . E*," I said. "The first word could be *he*."

"It could be, but I don't think so," Helen said. "The slash also appears in the third and the fifth words. The third word is *blank, blank, E, blank, E.* The fifth word is *blank, blank, E.*"

I sighed. "This is hard."

"Yes," Helen said happily. "It's a very good code. Look closely at the fifth word. The middle symbol is #, which is the same symbol between the two *E*s in the third word. Three vowels together in a word are rare, so the # must be a consonant. *T, N,* and *S* are the most common consonants in English, but *H* and *R* are common, too. For the fifth word, let's think of three-letter words that end in *E.*"

"There's *one.* There's *ate.*" I paused, thinking. "How about *the* and *are?*"

"A sentence wouldn't end with the word *the*," Helen said. "It could end with *one* or *are* or maybe *ate*. We also have to look at the third word. It would end with *ENE* or *ERE* or *ETE*."

"*Scene* or *there*?" I offered.

"Let's look at the first word again," Helen suggested. "It's *blank, E*."

"How about *W*?" I asked. "It's *we*!"

"You're right!" Helen exclaimed. "That means the third word is *W, blank, E, blank, E*."

"*Where*! I bet it's *where*!"

"Then the last word is *are*," Helen said. "So far, the sentence is *We blank where blank are*."

We compared the first two messages. The second message had a two-letter word with the symbols › and #. Since we knew that the # symbol was an *R*, the comma symbol had to be an *O*.

"*You*!" I shouted.

"What?" Helen looked surprised.

"Look at the first message! *We blank where blank are*! I think the fourth word is *you*!"

"And the second word has a *W* at the end. I'll bet it's *know*. *We know where you are*!" Helen exclaimed.

"We cracked the code!" I grabbed more drawings. "Let's figure out what these say."

We worked hard decoding the scribbles. Here's what we figured out:

KEEP QUIET OR ELSE

IF YOU TELL WE WILL BLAME YOU

DO NOT TELL ABOUT MISTRESS SMITH

"Who's writing these messages?" I asked.

Helen's eyes gleamed. "Whoever it is, they're not very friendly," she said.

18

Chapter 4

Uncovering the Clues

Later that morning, Helen and I went into the kitchen and found Mother pacing the floor.

"I don't know what to do with Lizzie," she snapped. "First, she scribbles on the wall, and now she's homesick."

"Lizzie didn't draw on the wall," Helen said.

Mother stopped pacing. "Then who did?"

"I don't know," Helen admitted. "But the drawings are actually messages, not scribbles."

Mother looked skeptical. "Even if that were true, I'd send Lizzie home anyway. She took all the books off the shelf in her room and built a castle. She's been jumping on the bed. She even tossed a set of blocks out the window."

"It sounds as if she's bored," I said.

"She'll have to be bored at home." Mother sighed. "Poor Trevor's been ill the whole visit. I thought about sending him home with his sister, but now he's too sick to travel. I sent word to the doctor to come by this afternoon."

My cousin had stayed in bed all morning, hardly eating anything and moaning a lot. I guessed he was more afraid than sick. We knew now that the scribbles were messages. They had started showing up when my cousins arrived, so Trevor and Lizzie must be connected to them.

Mother packed Lizzie's things, but there was a problem. Lizzie was too young to travel by herself, and Mother had to stay home and wait for the doctor to come.

Helen suggested that she and I accompany Lizzie back home. "We can ask her if she knows anything about the messages," she whispered.

Mother arranged for a carriage. Then she sent a telegram to Aunt Julia, telling her when to expect us. Soon, the three of us were bouncing along in the carriage, the horses trotting briskly.

"Lizzie, why did you jump on the bed?" Helen asked.

Lizzie shrugged. "It was fun."

"Is that why you built the book castle and threw the blocks out the window?" I asked.

Her eyes widened. "I threw the blocks because I was trying to hit the bad boy."

Helen looked at me, then back at Lizzie. "What bad boy?" she asked.

"The one drawing on the garden wall," Lizzie answered. "I tried to hit him with the blocks to make him stop. He was getting me in trouble."

This was exciting! Lizzie was an eyewitness! "Can you tell us what the boy looked like?" I asked.

"He tried to hide behind a tree, but he didn't fit," she said. Her eyes narrowed. "He looked like Rajiv. That's one of Trevor's friends. But how would he get here?"

"Perhaps on a horse," Helen answered. She wrote something in her notebook, then looked up again. "Lizzie, do you know who Mistress Smith is?"

I glanced at Helen. That was the name mentioned in the last message.

Lizzie nodded. "She's Trevor's teacher. Trevor doesn't like her because she's so hard."

I raised my eyebrows at Helen, who started scribbling in her notebook again.

⌇

We dropped Lizzie off at her house and talked to my Aunt Julia for a few minutes. We reassured her that Trevor would feel better soon. Then we asked for directions to Mistress Smith's house. I knew Aunt Julia was puzzled, but we weren't ready to give out too much information.

⌇

Mistress Smith lived just down the road, next to the woods and not far from Trevor's house. Her cottage needed painting and was surrounded by shrubs that needed trimming.

When we knocked, an older woman answered the door. We introduced ourselves to Mistress Smith.

Helen said, "We're trying to solve a mystery that might involve you. Has anything unusual happened to you recently?"

"Well, do you consider stealing unusual?" Mistress Smith asked. "Last weekend, someone stole my jewelry box. It contained two necklaces and three rings."

"Do many people know about this?" I asked.

She laughed. "This is a small town, young man. Everyone knows about it."

"What did your jewelry box look like?" Helen asked as she pulled out her notebook.

"It was a plain wooden box," Mistress Smith said. "I told the sheriff what happened, but he hasn't found anything yet. Does your mystery have to do with this theft?"

"We're not sure yet," I said.

"We plan to report to the sheriff anything we find out," Helen said. "Do you know how the thief broke into your house?"

"The thief didn't actually break in," Mistress Smith admitted. "I spent Saturday night with a sick friend. When I got home the next morning, I found I'd left my bedroom window open. You see, it had rained early Saturday evening. My dresser is under the window, and it was wet."

"Did you keep your jewelry box on the dresser?" I asked.

"How did you know?" she asked.

I grinned at Helen. I could be a good detective, too. "It would be easy to reach inside the window and take the jewelry box."

"I guess it would be," Mistress Smith said. She looked thoughtful. "No one has bothered me before, except for the schoolboys. I've heard them sneak up and make strange noises by my window, but that's just silly mischief. I knew who it was, though I never said anything."

"Would you show us the window?" Helen asked.

Mistress Smith led us around the side of her cottage. Helen pushed me over the bumpy yard. The flowers under the bedroom window were trampled. Helen examined the flower bed. She

checked the windowsill. She took a small piece of brown cloth from a nail in the window frame and tucked it into her notebook. ⚡

"Can you tell us the boys' names and where they live?" Helen asked. "We might want to talk to them."

Mistress Smith told us. We thanked her and walked away.

Instead of getting into the waiting carriage, Helen looked closely at the dirt road. Then she said, "John, I'm sorry to tell you that your cousin was involved in the theft of Mistress Smith's jewelry."

"That can't be!" I declared.

"The messages, the road, the flower bed, and this piece of cloth tell the tale."

I didn't want to admit it, but I had been growing suspicious, too. The cousin I knew would never steal, but Trevor hadn't been acting like the cousin I knew. "How can we find out for sure?" I asked.

"I have a plan" was all Helen said. ⚡

Chapter 5

Messages and Meetings

When we got back to my house early that evening, Mother was very upset. "I've made a terrible mistake," she said. "Lizzie definitely didn't make those drawings on the wall!"

"I agree," Helen said, nodding. "How did you come to that conclusion?"

"Long after the three of you left, I found new scribbles on the wall. It couldn't have been Lizzie. I was so unfair!" Mother cried.

"Where are the drawings?" I asked.

Mother shuddered. "I washed those horrible things away. Now that I know they're messages, they seem sinister."

Helen and I exchanged disappointed glances. We had lost a clue.

"How is Trevor feeling?" I asked.

"He doesn't seem any better," Mother said, frowning. "The doctor couldn't find anything wrong with him, but Trevor still claims his stomach hurts. It's very puzzling."

"Let's go talk to him," I said to Helen.

Trevor lay on his back in bed, staring at the ceiling. He hadn't gotten dressed all day. His oversized shoes lay on the floor where he'd left them the day before. I wheeled to a spot between his bed and the window.

"Mother says Lizzie wasn't to blame for the scribbles after all," I told Trevor.

He nodded without looking at me. If he was pretending to be sick, he was doing a good job. He certainly didn't look very well, but at least he had opened the draperies.

"What did the message say this time?" Helen asked.

Trevor jerked his head toward us. "I don't know what you're talking about!"

"We have a theory that the scribbles could be messages," Helen said. "Do you remember what this last one looked like?"

"How would I know? I can't see anything from here," Trevor argued. "I've been in bed all day. I'm sick." He turned away.

I sighed and glanced out the window, unhappy that Trevor wasn't talking. That's when I realized that he was lying.

With the draperies open, the garden wall was in plain sight from the extra bed. Trevor would have been able to see any message written on it without ever having to leave his bed.

I'd been hoping that Trevor wasn't really guilty, but now I knew he'd been involved. Why else would he lie?

I motioned to Helen to look out the window. She glanced outside and frowned.

We left the room, and I whispered, "Did you notice the wall?"

Helen tapped her notebook. "It's time to get Trevor to show that he knows the code."

I helped Helen compose a message in code. It read, *Meet us at the garden gate right now or else.* I waited in my room until Trevor left to get a drink. Then I signaled to Helen outside, who wrote the message on the wall.

Just as we'd planned, Trevor saw the message when he returned and ran straight to the gate. I wheeled after him. Helen was already there, waiting for us.

"Are you ready to tell us about the messages?" she asked.

Trevor frowned. "That was a mean trick."

"Any meaner than letting your sister take the blame for the scribbles?" I asked.

He stared at the ground. "I didn't know what else to do. Yes, I know the code. I invented it. It was just for fun—a way for my friends and me to send secret messages."

He broke a twig from the tree, then snapped it again and again. The pieces dropped to the ground.

"Tell us what's going on," I urged. "Did you hide the jewelry?"

"Yes! I mean, no! Oh, you've read the messages. I can't tell anybody anything!" Trevor turned around and ran back to the house.

"He's really scared," I said.

"*Keep quiet or else,*" Helen repeated one of the messages. "That's a threat. It's time to talk to Uncle Sherlock."

That evening, Sherlock Holmes helped us contact the sheriff in Trevor's town. We arranged for the sheriff and his men to meet us in the woods near Mistress Smith's cottage the next afternoon.

Now that we knew where they lived, we sent both of Trevor's friends a coded message. The message read, *Meet tomorrow at 3 P.M. where we hid the jewelry, or else!*

The next morning, we wrote that message on the garden wall. When Trevor saw it from the window, he ran to the parlor where Mother was reading. Helen and I were working on a crossword puzzle.

"Aunt Margaret, I have to go home!" he said.

"But Trevor, you don't look a bit better," Mother told him.

"I'll feel better in my own bed," he insisted.

I could tell Mother didn't want to let him go, but finally she gave in. "All right, then. I'll arrange for a carriage," she said with a sigh.

Trevor pointed out that going by horseback would be faster, but Mother wouldn't hear of it. "You're too sick," she said. "I don't even want you in the carriage alone."

"We'll go with him," Helen offered.

Trevor looked worried the whole way home. We tried talking to him, but he wouldn't answer any questions. When we dropped him off at his house, we knew he wouldn't stay there long.

As soon as we were out of sight of Trevor's house, we got out of the carriage. We waited patiently in the shadows of a barn until we saw Trevor sneak out of his house. He walked quickly toward Mistress Smith's cottage. We followed at a distance, keeping to the shadows.

Trevor entered the woods behind Mistress Smith's home and walked down a path. Helen pushed my wheelchair over the rough ground. We could hear voices ahead of us.

"All right, I'm here," Trevor said. "What do you want?"

"We didn't call this meeting," a voice said. "You did."

"Not me," Trevor said in surprise. "What's going on?"

Helen pushed my wheelchair into a clearing where Trevor stood with two boys.

"We called this meeting," she announced.

Chapter 6

Solving the Secret

"What's going on?" one of the boys asked angrily. "Who are you?"

Sheriff Tate and his men stepped out from their hiding places. "You should recognize us, Rajiv," he said.

All three boys stepped back, their mouths open in surprise. The red-haired boy, Kevin, started to run, but the sheriff grabbed him.

"Sheriff, these boys stole Mistress Smith's jewelry," Helen announced. "It wasn't a planned robbery. It was a prank that went wrong."

Sheriff Tate stared at Helen. "How could you know it was a prank from the evidence you gave me?" he asked.

Indeed, I'd seen the same clues as Helen, but I hadn't come to the same conclusion. I thought Trevor and his friends wanted revenge for their hard school year.

Helen whipped out her notebook. "Follow me toward Mistress Smith's window, and I'll show you how I put it all together," she said.

Helen stopped in the road near the house and pointed to impressions in the dried mud.

"Trevor and his friends came here Saturday after the rain had stopped," Helen began.

Trevor interrupted her. "Those could be anybody's footprints."

Helen smiled and pointed to his feet. "You have the biggest feet I've ever seen. Put your foot in this footprint and see if it matches."

When Trevor quickly backed away, I knew the footprints must be his.

"You and your friends had tried to scare Mistress Smith on other occasions by making noises outside her window," Helen continued.

"How did you know that?" Rajiv asked.

"Watch what you say, Rajiv!" Kevin muttered.

Helen interrupted them. "Trevor's footprints stop here. He stood at this spot for some time, and he was quite nervous."

"You can tell all that from footprints?" I asked.

Helen bent down and pointed at the ground nearby. "Look at this pile of broken twigs."

I nodded. Trevor's nervous habit had given him away. "Then Trevor didn't go near Mistress Smith's window!" I exclaimed, relieved.

"I think he stayed back here on the road as a lookout," Helen said.

"Maybe he was just standing in the road snapping sticks," Kevin muttered.

"Oh, no, Trevor wasn't alone," Helen said. "Let's continue our study under the window."

Helen led the group to the shrubs next to the house. "The flower bed has been trampled. I see two different kinds of prints."

"That doesn't mean it was Kevin and me," Rajiv said.

"Some prints are much deeper than others. They're too deep for one boy to make—unless someone was riding on his shoulders!"

Both boys' eyes widened in amazement.

Helen produced the brown cloth she'd taken from beneath the window ledge. "This is a scrap I found caught on that nail. It was torn from Kevin's sleeve."

Kevin clapped his hand over his left sleeve, but it was too late. The group had already seen the tear in his brown jacket.

"Why did you have to wear that jacket again?" Rajiv groaned.

"I'm lucky I'm still alive, the way you stumbled!" Kevin cried. "When you fell over, I could've broken my neck!"

Helen looked pleased with herself. "Kevin was riding on Rajiv's shoulders. They wanted to scare Mistress Smith."

"They'd tried to scare her before," I said.

"Right," Helen said. "But this time, Rajiv stumbled and fell in the mud. You can see where he smashed these plants. As Rajiv fell, Kevin threw his arms out to grab onto something. He aimed for the dresser but got only the jewelry box, knocking it to the ground as he fell."

"We thought we heard her coming home," Rajiv added. "That's why I fell in the mud."

Helen turned to the boys. "Not knowing what to do, you grabbed the box and ran away. You didn't know until you opened the box in the woods that you had stolen some jewelry."

Trevor almost looked relieved. "You're right!" he exclaimed.

"Good work, Helen!" Sheriff Tate was impressed. He turned to Trevor and the other boys. "When you saw it was jewelry, why didn't you put it back?"

"We were scared," Trevor said. "Kevin said we should bury it. He's the one who grabbed it in the first place, so we listened to him."

"Well, you didn't have a better idea," Kevin replied, glaring at Trevor.

"We only wanted to scare her," Rajiv said.

Helen closed her notebook. "Let's go back to the woods." She led our group back the way we'd come, stopping beside a tall tree.

"Where is the box?" I asked.

Helen kneeled down next to a small mound of dirt with several large rocks on top.

"That's the place," Trevor said.

I suddenly remembered what Lizzie had told us about the boy in the yard. "Rajiv, you followed Trevor to my house," I said.

"Yes, I did," Rajiv admitted. "When Trevor left, we were worried that he'd turn us in. I rode my horse to your town every day. That way, I could spy on Trevor to make sure he kept our secret."

"What were you planning to do with the jewelry?" Sheriff Tate asked the boys.

Kevin shrugged. "I guess we figured we'd put it back. You know, sneak it in the open window when Mistress Smith wasn't looking."

"How about taking it back to her now?" Sheriff Tate suggested.

The boys started digging and pulled out the box. When we reached Mistress Smith's cottage, Trevor and his friends told her they were sorry.

"You should all go to jail," Sheriff Tate said. "But Mistress Smith has convinced me to do something different."

"My house needs painting, and my garden needs weeding," the boys' teacher said.

The boys looked sheepish but relieved. Trevor turned to me.

"I'm sorry for the way I acted," he said. "I wasn't very nice to you or Lizzie, and I really upset Aunt Margaret. I'd like to come back and say I'm sorry in person. Then maybe we could have the visit we'd originally planned."

"That's a good idea," I agreed.

On the way home, I told Helen, "That was amazing! How do you do it?"

"It's simple," Helen said. "I observe, as Uncle Sherlock taught me. It's a nice hobby, and it keeps me from getting bored."

I laughed. Life was definitely never boring with Helen.